EARLY TALES AND SKETCHES

EARLY TALES AND SKETCHES

BJÖRNSTJERNE BJÖRNSON

Translated from the Norse

By

RASMUS B. ANDERSON

Fredonia Books
Amsterdam, The Netherlands

Early Tales and Sketches

by
Björnstjerne Björnson

ISBN: 1-4101-0333-1

Reprinted from the 1882 edition

Fredonia Books
Amsterdam, The Netherlands
http://www.fredoniabooks.com

In order to make original editions of historical works available to scholars at an economical price, this facsimile of the original edition of 1882 is reproduced from the best available copy and has been digitally enhanced to improve legibility, but the text remains unaltered to retain historical authenticity.

EARLY TALES AND SKETCHES

CONTENTS

THE RAILROAD AND THE CHURCHYARD.

CHAPTER I.

KNUD AAKRE belonged to an old family in the parish, where it had always been renowned for its intelligence and its devotion to the public welfare. His father had worked his way up to the priesthood, but had died early, and as the widow came from a peasant stock, the children were brought up as peasants. Knud had, therefore, received only the education afforded by the public schools of his day; but his father's library had early inspired him with a love of knowledge. This was further stimulated by his friend Henrik Wergeland, who frequently visited him, sent him books, seeds, and much valuable counsel. Following some of the latter, Knud early founded a club, which in the beginning had a very miscellaneous object, for instance: " to give the members prac-

tice in debating and to study the constitution,"
but which later was turned into a practical
agricultural society for the entire bailiwick.
According to Wergeland's advice, he also
founded a parish library, giving his father's
books as its first endowment. A suggestion
from the same quarter led him to start a Sunday-
school on his gard, for those who might wish to
learn writing, arithmetic, and history. All this
drew attention to him, so that he was elected
member of the parish board of supervisors, of
which he soon became chairman. In this ca-
pacity, he took a deep interest in the schools,
which he brought into a remarkably good con-
dition.

Knud Aakre was a short man, brisk in his
movements, with small, restless eyes and very
disorderly hair. He had large lips, which were
in constant motion, and a row of splendid teeth
which always seemed to be working with them,
for they glistened while his words were snapped
out, crisp and clear, crackling like sparks from
a great fire.

Foremost among the many he had helped to
gain an education was his neighbor Lars Högstad. Lars was not much younger than Knud,
but he had developed more slowly. Knud
liked to talk about what he read and thought,

and he found in Lars, whose manner was quiet and grave, a good listener, who by degrees grew to be a man of excellent judgment. The relations between them soon became such that Knud was never willing to take any important step without first consulting Lars Högstad, and the matter on hand was thus likely to gain some practical amendment. So Knud drew his neighbor into the board of supervisors, and gradually into everything in which he himself took part. They always drove together to the meetings of the board, where Lars never spoke; but on the way back and forth Knud learned his opinions. The two were looked upon as inseparable.

One fine autumn day the board of supervisors convened to consider, among other things, a proposal from the bailiff to sell the parish grain magazine and with the proceeds establish a small savings-bank. Knud Aakre, the chairman, would undoubtedly have approved this measure had he relied on his unbiased judgment. But he was prejudiced, partly because the proposal came from the bailiff, whom Wergeland did not like, and who was consequently no favorite of Knud's either, and partly because the grain magazine had been built by his influential paternal grandfather and by him presented to the parish. Indeed, Knud was rather inclined to view the proposition as a personal insult, therefore he had not spoken of it to any one, not even to Lars, and the latter never entered on a topic that had not first been set afloat by some one else.

As chairman, Knud Aakre read the proposal without adding any comments; but, as was his wont, his eyes sought Lars, who usually sat or stood a little aside, holding a straw between his teeth, — he always had one when he took part in a conversation; he either used it as a tooth-pick, or he let it hang loosely in one corner of his mouth, turning it more rapidly or more slowly, according to the mood he was in. To his surprise Knud saw that the straw was moving very fast.

"Do you think we should agree to this?" he asked, quickly.

Lars answered, dryly, —

"Yes, I do."

The whole board, feeling that Knud held quite a different opinion, looked in astonishment at Lars, but the latter said no more, nor was he further questioned. Knud turned to another matter, as though nothing had transpired. Not until the close of the meeting did he resume the subject, and then asked, with apparent indifference, if it would not be well to send the proposal back to the bailiff for further consideration, as it certainly did not meet the views of the people, for the parish valued the grain magazine. No one replied. Knud asked whether he should enter the resolution in the register, the measure did not seem to be a wise one.

" Against one vote," added Lars.

" Against two," cried another, promptly.

" Against three," came from a third; and before the chairman could realize what was taking place, a majority had voted in favor of the proposal.

Knud was so surprised that he forgot to offer any opposition. He recorded the proceedings and read, in a low voice: " The measure is recommended, — adjourned."

His face was fiery red as he rose and put up the minute-book; but he determined to bring forward the question once more at the meeting of the representatives. Out in the yard, he put his horse to the wagon, and Lars came and took his seat at his side. They discussed various topics on their way home, but not the one they had nearest at heart.

The next day Knud's wife sought Lars's wife to inquire if there was anything wrong between

the two men, for Knud had acted so strangely
when he came home.   A short distance above
the gard buildings she met Lars's wife, who was
on her way to ask the same question, for her
husband, too, had been out of sorts the day before.   Lars's wife was a quiet, bashful person,
somewhat cowed, not by harsh words, but by
silence, for Lars never spoke to her unless she
had done something amiss, or he feared that
she might do wrong.   Knud Aakre's wife, on the
other hand, talked more with her husband, and
particularly about the board, for lately it had
taken his thoughts, work, and affection away
from her and the children.   She was as jealous
of it as of a woman ; she wept at night over the
board and quarreled with her husband about
it during the day.   But for that very reason
she could say nothing about it now when for
once he had returned home unhappy ; for she
immediately became more wretched than he,
and for her life she could not rest until she had
discovered what was the matter.   Consequently,
when Lars's wife could not give her the desired
information, she had to go out in the parish to
seek it.   Here she obtained it, and of course
was at once of her husband's opinion ; she found
Lars incomprehensible, not to say wicked.
When, however, she let her husband perceive

this, she felt that as yet there was no breach between Lars and him ; that, on the contrary, he clung warmly to him.

The representatives met. Lars Högstad drove over to Aakre in the morning ; Knud came out of the house and took his seat beside him. They exchanged the usual greetings, spoke perhaps rather less than was their wont on the way, and not of the proposal.   All the members of the board were present; some, too, had found their way in as spectators, which Knud did not like, for it showed that there was a stir in town about the matter. Lars was armed with his straw, and he stood by the stove warming himself, for the autumn was beginning to be cold.   The chairman read the proposal, in a subdued, cautious manner, remarking when he was through, that it must be remembered this came from the bailiff, who was not apt to be very felicitous in his propositions.   The building, it was well known, was a gift, and it is not customary to part with gifts, least of all when there is no need of doing so.

Lars, who never before had spoken at the meetings, now took the floor, to the astonishment of all. His voice trembled, but whether it did so out of regard for Knud, or from anxiety lest his own cause should be lost, shall remain unsaid.   But his arguments were good and clear, and full of a logic and confidence which had scarcely been heard at these meetings before.   And when he had gone over all the ground, he added, in conclusion : —

"What does it matter if the proposal does come from the bailiff?   This affects the question as little as who erected the building, or in what way it came into the public possession."

Knud Aakre had grown very red in the face (he blushed easily), and he shifted uneasily from side to side, as was his wont when he was impatient, but none the less did he exert himself to be circumspect and to speak in a low voice.   There were savings-banks enough in the country, he thought, and quite near at hand, he might almost say *too* near.   But if, after all, it was deemed expedient to have one, there were surely other ways of reaching it than those leading over the gifts of the dead and the love of the living.   His voice was a little unsteady when he said this, but quickly recovered as he proceeded to speak of the grain magazine in itself, and to show what its advantages were.

Lars answered him thoroughly on the last point, and then added, —

"However, one thing and another lead me to doubt whether this parish is managed for the sake of the living or the dead; furthermore, whether it is the love and hatred of a single family which controls matters here, or the good of the whole."

Knud answered quickly, —

"I do not know whether he who has just spoken has been least benefited by this family, — both by the dead and by him who now lives."

The first shot was aimed at the fact that Knud's powerful grandfather had saved the gard for Lars's paternal grandfather, when the latter, on his part, was absent on a little excursion to the penitentiary.

The straw which long had been in brisk motion, suddenly became still.

"It is not my way to keep talking everywhere about myself and my family," said Lars, then turned again with calm superiority to the subject under discussion, briefly reviewing all the points with one definite object. Knud had to admit to himself that he had never viewed the matter from such a broad standpoint; involuntarily he raised his eyes and looked at Lars, who stood before him, tall, heavily built, with clearness on the vigorous brow and in the deep eyes. The lips were tightly compressed, the straw still played in the corner of his mouth; all the surrounding lines indicated vigor. He kept his hands behind him, and stood rigidly erect, while his voice was as deep and as hollow as if it proceeded from the depths of the earth. For the first time in his life Knud saw him as he was, and in his inmost soul he was afraid of him; for this man must always have been his superior. He had taken all Knud himself knew and could impart; he had rejected the tares and retained what had produced this strong, hidden growth.

He had been fostered and loved by Knud, but had now become a giant who hated Knud deeply, terribly. Knud could not explain to himself why, but as he looked at Lars he instinctively felt this to be so, and all else becoming swallowed up in this thought he started up, exclaiming, —

"But Lars! Lars! what in Heaven's name is the matter with you?" His agitation overcame him, — "you, whom I have — you who have" —

Powerless to utter another word, he sat down; but in his effort to gain the mastery over the emotion he deemed Lars unworthy of seeing, he brought his fist down with violence on the table, while his eyes flashed beneath his stiff, disorderly hair, which always hung over them. Lars acted as if he had not been interrupted, and turning toward the others he asked if this was to be the decisive blow; for if such were the case there was no need for further remarks.

This calmness was more than Knud could endure.

"What is it that has come among us?" cried he. "We who have, until to-day, been actuated by love and zeal alone, are now stirred up against each other, as though goaded on by some evil spirit," and he cast a fiery glance at Lars, who replied, —

"It must be you yourself who bring in this spirit, Knud; for I have kept strictly to the matter before us. But you never can see the advantage of anything you do not want yourself; now we shall learn what becomes of the love and the zeal when once this matter is decided as we wish."

"Have I then illy served the interests of the parish?"

There was no reply. This grieved Knud, and he continued, —

"I really did persuade myself that I had accomplished various things — various things which have been of advantage to the parish; but perhaps I have deceived myself."

He was again overcome by his feelings; for his was a fiery nature, ever variable in its moods, and the breach with Lars pained him so deeply that he could scarcely control himself. Lars answered, —

"Yes, I know you appropriate the credit for all that is done here, and if one should judge by the amount of speaking at these meetings, you certainly have accomplished the most."

"Is that the way of it?" shouted Knud, looking sharply at Lars. "It is you who deserve the entire honor?"

"Since we must finally talk about ourselves," said Lars, "I am free to admit that every question has been carefully considered by both of us before it was introduced here."

Here little Knud Aakre regained his ready speech: —

"Take the honor, in God's name; I am quite able to live without it; there are other things that are harder to lose!"

Involuntarily Lars evaded his gaze, but said, as he set the straw in very rapid motion, —

"If I were to express *my* opinion, I should say that there is not very much to take credit for. No doubt the priest and the school-masters are content with what has been done; but certainly the common people say that up to the present time the taxes of this parish have grown heavier and heavier."

Here arose a murmur in the crowd, and the people grew very restless.   Lars continued, —

" Finally, to-day we have a matter brought before us that might make the parish some little amends for all it has paid out ; this is perhaps the reason why it encounters such opposition.   This is a question which concerns the parish ; it is for the welfare of all ; it is our duty to protect it from becoming a mere family matter."

People exchanged glances, and spoke in half-audible tones ; one of them remarked, as he rose to go for his dinner-pail, that these were the truest words he had heard in these meetings for many years.   Now all rose from their seats, the conversation became general, and Knud Aakre, who alone remained sitting, felt that all was lost, fearfully lost, and made no further effort to save it.   The truth was, he possessed something of the temperament attributed to Frenchmen : he was very good at a first, second, or even third attack, but poor at self-defense, for his sensibilities overwhelmed his thoughts.

He was unable to comprehend this, nor could he sit still any longer, and so resigning his place to the vice-chairman, he left.   The others could not refrain from a smile.

He had come to the meeting in company with Lars, but went home alone, although the way was long. It was a cold autumn day, the forest was jagged and bare, the meadow gray-yellow, frost was beginning here and there to remain on the road-side. Disappointment is a terrible companion.   Knud felt so small, so desolate, as he walked along; but Lars appeared everywhere before him, towering up to the sky, in the dusk of the evening, like a giant.   It vexed him to think it was his own fault that this had been the decisive battle; he had staked too much on one single little issue.   But surprise, pain, anger, had mastered him; they still burned, tingled, moaned, and stormed within him. He heard the rumbling of cart-wheels behind him; it was Lars driving his superb horse past him, in a brisk trot, making the hard road resound like distant thunder. Knud watched the broad-shouldered form that sat erect in the cart, while the horse, eager for home, sped onward, without any effort on the part of Lars, who merely gave him a loose rein.   It was but a picture of this man's power: he was driving onward to the goal!   Knud felt himself cast out of his eart, to stagger on alone in the chill autumn air.

In his home at Aakre Knud's wife was waiting for him. She knew that a battle was inevit-
ble; she had never in her life trusted Lars, and
now she was positively afraid of him. It had
been no comfort to her that he and her husband
had driven away together; it would not have
consoled her had they returned in the same way.
But darkness had fallen and they had not come.
She stood in the doorway, gazing out on the
road in front of the house; she walked down the
hill and back again, but no cart appeared.

Finally she hears a rattling on the hard
road, her heart throbs as the wheels go round,
she clings to the casement, peering out into the
night; the cart draws near; only one is in it;
she recognizes Lars, who sees and recognizes
her, but drives past without stopping. Now she
became thoroughly alarmed. Her limbs gave
way under her, she tottered in and sank down
on the bench by the window. The children
gathered anxiously about her, the youngest one
asked for papa; she never spoke with them but
of him. He had such a noble disposition, and
this was what made her love him; but now his
heart was not with his family, it was engrossed
in all sorts of business which brought him only
unhappiness, and consequently they were all
unhappy.

If only no misfortune had befallen him !
Knud was so hot-tempered. Why had Lars
come home alone? Why did he not stop?
Should she run after him, or down the road
after her husband? She was in an agony of dis-
tress, and the children pressed around her, ask-
ing what was the matter. But this she would
not tell them, so rising she said they must eat
supper alone, then got everything ready and
helped them. All the while she kept glancing
out on the road. He did not come. She undressed the children and put them to bed, and
the youngest repeated the evening prayer while
she bowed over him. She herself prayed with
such fervor in the words which the infant lips
so soothingly uttered that she did not heed the
steps outside.

Knud stood upon the threshold, gazing at his
little company at prayer. The mother drew
herself up; all the children shouted: " Papa! "
but he seated himself at once, and said, softly:

" Oh, let him say it once more! "

The mother turned again to the bedside, that
he, meanwhile, should not see her face, for it
would have seemed like intruding on his grief
before he felt the need of revealing it. The
little one folded its hands over its breast, all
the rest did likewise, and it repeated, —

> " I, a little child, pray Heaven
>   That my sins may be forgiven,
>   With time I 'll larger, wiser grow,
>   And my father and mother joy shall know,
>   If only Thou, dearest, dearest Lord,
>   Will help me to keep Thy precious word !
>   And now to our Heavenly Father's merciful keeping
>   Our souls let us trust while we 're sleeping."

What peace now fell upon the room ! Not a minute had elapsed ere all the children were sleeping as in the arms of God ; but the mother moved softly away and placed supper before the father, who was, however, unable to eat. But after he had gone to bed, he said, —

" Henceforth I shall be at home."

And his wife lay at his side trembling with joy which she dared not betray ; and she thanked God for all that had happened, for whatever it might be it had resulted in good !

CHAPTER II.

IN the course of a year Lars had become chairman of the parish board of supervisors, president of the savings-bank, and leading commissioner in the court of reconciliation ; in short, he held every office to which his election had been possible. In the board of supervisors for

the amt (county) he was silent during the first
year, but the second year he created the same
sensation when he spoke as in the parish board;
for here, too, coming forward in opposition to
him who had previously been the guiding
power, he became victorious over the entire
rank and file and was from that time himself
the leader. From this his path led him to the
storthing (parliament), where his fame had
preceded him, and where consequently there
was no lack of challenges. But here, although
steady and firm, he always remained retiring.
He did not care for power except where he was
well known, nor would he endanger his leader-
ship at home by a possible defeat abroad.

For he had a pleasant life at home. When
he stood by the church wall on Sundays, and
the congregation walked slowly past, saluting
him and stealing side glances at him, and one
after another paused in order to exchange a
few words with him, — then truly it might be
said that he controlled the entire parish with a
straw, for of course this hung in the corner of
his mouth.

He deserved his honors. The road leading
to the church, he had opened; the new church
they were standing beside, he had built; this
and much more was the fruit of the savings

bank which he had founded and now managed himself. For its resources were further made fruitful, and the parish was constantly held up as an example to all others of self-management and good order.

Knud Aakre had entirely withdrawn from the field, although at first he attended a few of the meetings of the board, because he had promised himself that he would continue to offer his services, even if it were not altogether pleasing to his pride. In the first proposal he had made, he became so greatly perplexed by Lars, who insisted upon having it represented in all its details, that, somewhat hurt, he said: "When Columbus discovered America he did not have it divided into parishes and deaneries; this came gradually;" whereupon Lars, in his reply, compared the discovery of America with Knud's proposal, — it so happened that this treated of stable improvements, — and afterwards Knud was known by no other name in the board than " Discovery of America." So Knud thought that as his usefulness had ceased, so too had his obligations to work, and he refused to accept further reëlections.

But he continued to be industrious; and in order that he might still have a field for usefulness, he enlarged his Sunday-school, and placed it, by means of small contributions from the attendants, in communication with the mission cause, of which he soon became the centre and leader in his own and the surrounding counties. Thereupon Lars Högstad remarked, that if ever Knud undertook to collect money for any purpose, he must know beforehand that it was to do good thousands of miles from home.

There was, be it observed, no more strife between them. To be sure, they no longer associated with each other, but they bowed and spoke when they met. Knud always felt a little pain at the mere thought of Lars, but strove to suppress it, and persuade himself that matters could not have been otherwise. At a large wedding-party, many years afterward, where both were present and both were in good spirits, Knud mounted a chair and proposed a toast for the chairman of the parish board, and the first representative their amt had sent to the storthing! He spoke until he became deeply moved, and, as usual, expressed himself in an exceedingly handsome way. Every one thought it was honorably done, and Lars came up to him, and his gaze was unsteady as he said that for much of what he knew and was he was indebted to him.

At the next election of the board of supervisors Knud was again made chairman !

But had Lars Högstad foreseen what now
followed, he would certainly not have used his
influence for this. "Every event happens in its
own time," says an old proverb, and just as
Knud Aakre again entered the board, the best
men of the parish were threatened with ruin,
as the result of a speculation craze which had
long been raging, but which now first began to
demand its victims. It was said that Lars Högstad was the cause of this great disaster, for he
had taught the parish to speculate. This penny
fever had originated in the parish board of
supervisors, for the board itself was the greatest speculator of all. Every one down to the
laboring youth of twenty years desired in his
transactions to make ten dollars out of one; a
beginning of extreme avarice in the efforts to
hoard, was followed by an excessive extrava-
gance, and as all minds were bent only on money, there had at the same time developed a
spirit of suspicion, of intolerance, of caviling,
which resulted in lawsuits and hatred. This
also was due to the example of the board, it
was said, for among the first things Lars had
done as chairman was to sue the venerable old
priest for holding doubtful titles. The priest

had lost, but had also immediately resigned.
At that time some had praised, some censured
this suit; but it had proved a bad example.
Now came the consequences of Lars's manage-
ment, in the form of loss to every single man
of property in the parish, consequently public
opinion underwent a sharp change! The op-
posing force, too, soon found a leader, for Knud
Aakre had come into the board, introduced
there by Lars himself!

The struggle began forthwith. All those
youths to whom Knud in his time had given
instructions, were now grown up and were the
most enlightened men in the parish, thoroughly at home in all its transactions and public
affairs. It was against these men that Lars
now had to contend, and they had borne him a
grudge from their childhood up. When of an
evening after one of these stormy proceedings
he stood on the steps in front of his house, gazing over the parish, he could hear a sound as
of distant rumbling thunder rising toward him
from the large gards, now lying in the storm.
He knew that the day they met their ruin,
the savings-bank and himself would be over-
thrown, and all his long efforts would culminate
in imprecations heaped on his head.

In these days of conflict and despair, a party

of railroad commissioners, who were to survey
the route for a new road, made their appear-
ance one evening at Högstad, the first gard at
the entrance to the parish.   In the course of
conversation during the evening, Lars learned
that there was a question whether the road
should run through this valley or another par-
allel to it.

Like a flash of lightning it darted through
his mind that if he could succeed in having it
laid here, all property would rise in value, and
not only would he himself be saved but his fame
would be transmitted to the latest posterity!
He could not sleep that night, for his eyes were
dazzled by a glowing light, and sometimes he
could even hear the sound of the cars.   The
next day he went himself with the commissioners while they examined the locality; his
horse took them, and to his gard they returned.
The next day they drove through the other
valley; he was still with them, and he drove
them back again to his house.   They found a
brilliant illumination at Högstad; the first men
of the parish had been invited to be present at
a magnificent party given in honor of the
commissioners; it lasted until morning.   But
to no avail, for the nearer they came to a final
issue, the more plainly it appeared that the

road could not pass through this locality without undue expense. The entrance to the valley lay through a narrow gorge, and just as it swung into the parish, the swollen river swung in also, so that the railroad would either have to take the same curve along the mountain that the highway now made, thus running at a needlessly high altitude and crossing the river twice, or it would have to run straight forward, and thus through the old, now unused churchyard. Now the church had but recently been removed, and it was not long since the last burial had taken place there.

If it only depended on a bit of old churchyard, thought Lars, whether or not this great blessing came into the parish, then he must use his name and his energy for the removal of this obstacle! He at once set forth on a visit to the priest and the dean, and furthermore to the diocese council; he talked and he negotiated, for he was armed with all possible facts concerning the immense advantage of the railroad on one hand, and the sentiments of the parish on the other, and actually succeeded in winning all parties. It was promised him that by a removal of part of the bodies to the new churchyard the objections might be considered set aside, and the royal permission obtained for the churchyard to be taken for the line of railroad. It was told him that nothing was now needed but for him to set the question afloat in the board of supervisors.

The parish had grown as excited as himself : the spirit of speculation which for many years had been the only one prevailing in the parish, now became madly jubilant. There was nothing spoken or thought of but Lars's journey and its possible results. When he returned with the most magnificent promises, they made much of him ; songs were sung in his praise ; indeed, if at that time the largest gards had gone to destruction, one after another, no one would have paid the slightest attention to it : the speculation craze had given way to the railroad craze.

The board of supervisors assembled : there was presented for approval a respectful petition, that the old churchyard might be appropriated as the route of the railroad. This was unanimously adopted ; there was even mention of giving Lars a vote of thanks and a coffee-pot in the form of a locomotive. But it was finally thought best to wait until the whole plan was carried into execution. The petition came back from the diocese council, with a demand for a list of all bodies that would have to be removed. The priest made out such a list, but in-

stead of sending it direct, he had his own reasons
for sending it through the parish board. One
of the members carried it to the next meeting.
Here it fell to the lot of Lars, as chairman, to
open the envelope and read the list.

Now it chanced that the first body to be dis-
interred was that of Lars's own grandfather! A
little shudder ran through the assembly! Lars
himself was startled, but nevertheless continued
to read. Then it furthermore chanced that the
second body was that of Knud Aakre's grandfather, for these two men had died within a
short time of each other. Knud Aakre sprang
from his seat; Lars paused; every one looked
up in consternation, for old Knud Aakre had
been the benefactor of the parish and its best
beloved man, time out of mind. There was a
dead silence, which lasted for some minutes. At
last Lars cleared his throat and went on reading. But the further he proceeded the worse
the matter grew; for the nearer they came to
their own time, the dearer were the dead.
When he had finished, Knud Aakre asked
quietly whether the others did not agree with
him in thinking that the air about them was
filled with spirits. It was just beginning to
grow dark in the room, and although they were
mature men and were sitting in numbers to-

gether, they could not refrain from feeling alarmed. Lars produced a bundle of matches from his pocket and struck a light, dryly remarking, that this was no more than they knew beforehand.

"Yes, it is," said Knud pacing the floor, "it is more than I knew before. Now I begin to think that even railroads can be purchased too dearly."

These words sent a quiver through the audience, and observing that they had better further consider the matter, Knud made a motion to that effect.

" In the excitement which had prevailed," he said, " the benefit likely to be derived from the road had been overestimated. Even if the railroad did not pass through this parish, there would have to be stations at both ends of the valley; true, it would always be a little more troublesome to drive to them than to a station right in our midst; yet the difficulty would not be so very great that it would be necessary because of it to violate the repose of the dead."

Knud was one of those who when his thoughts were once in rapid motion could present the most convincing arguments; a moment before what he now said had not occurred to his mind, nevertheless it struck home to all.

Lars felt the danger of his position, and con-
cluding that it was best to be cautious, ap-
parently acquiesced in Knud's proposition to
reconsider. Such emotions are always worse
in the beginning, he thought; it is wisest to
temporize with them.

But he had miscalculated. In ever increasing waves the dread of touching the dead of
their own families swept over the inhabitants
of the parish; what none of them had thought
of as long as the matter existed merely in the
abstract, now became a serious question when it
was brought home to themselves. The women
especially were excited, and the road near the
court-house was black with people the day of
the next meeting. It was a warm summer day,
the windows were removed, and there were as
many without the house as within. All felt
that a great battle was about to be fought.

Lars came driving up with his handsome
horse, and was greeted by all; he looked calmly
and confidently around, not seeming to be surprised at anything. He took a seat near the
window, found his straw, and a suspicion of a
smile played over his keen face as he saw Knud
Aakre rise to his feet to act as spokesman for
all the dead in the old Högstad churchyard.

But Knud Aakre did not begin with the

churchyard. He began with an accurate exposition of how greatly the profits likely to accrue from having the railroad run through the parish had been overestimated in all this turmoil. He had positive proofs for every statement he made, for he had calculated the distance of each gard from the nearest station, and finally he asked, —

"Why has there been so much ado about this railroad, if not in behalf of the parish?"

This he could easily explain to them. There were those who had occasioned so great a disturbance that a still greater one was required to conceal it. Moreover, there were those who in the first outburst of excitement could sell their gards and belongings to strangers who were foolish enough to purchase. It was a shameful speculation which not only the living but the dead must serve to promote!

The effect of his address was very considerable. But Lars had once for all resolved to preserve his composure let come what would. He replied, therefore, with a smile, that he had been under the impression that Knud himself was eager for the railroad, and certainly no one would accuse him of having any knowledge of speculation. (Here followed a little laugh.) Knud had not evinced the slightest objection to

the removal of the bodies of common people for
the sake of the railroad; but when his own
grandfather's body was in question then it suddenly affected the welfare of the whole com-
munity! He said no more, but looked with a
faint smile at Knud, as did also several others.
Meanwhile, Knud Aakre surprised both him
and them by replying:—

"I confess it; I did not comprehend the
matter until it touched my own family feelings; it is possible that this may be a shame,
but it would have been a far greater one not
to have realized it at last — as is the case with
Lars! Never," he concluded, "could this rail-
lery have been more out of place; for to people with common decency the whole affair is
absolutely revolting."

"This feeling is something that has come up
quite recently," replied Lars, "we may therefore hope that it will soon pass over again.
May it not perhaps help the matter a little to
think what the priest, dean, diocese council, en-
gineers, and government will all say if we first
unanimously set the ball in motion, then come
and beg to have it stopped? If we first are
jubilant and sing songs, then weep and deliver
funeral orations? If they do not say that we
have gone mad in this parish, they must at all

events say that we have acted rather strangely of late."

"Yes, God knows, they may well think so!" replied Knud. "We have, indeed, acted very strangely of late, and it is high time for us to mend our ways. Things have come to a serious pass when we can each disinter his own grandfather to make way for a railroad; when we can disturb the resting-place of the dead in order that our own burdens may the more easily be carried. For is not this rooting in our churchyard in order to make it yield us food the same thing? What is buried there in the name of Jesus, we take up in Moloch's name — this is but little better than eating the bones of our ancestors."

"Such is the course of nature," said Lars, dryly.

"Yes, of plants and of animals."

"And are not we animals?"

"We are, but also the children of the living God, who have buried our dead in faith in Him: it is He who shall rouse them and not we."

"Oh, you are talking idly! Are we not obliged to have the graves dug up at any rate, when their turn comes? What harm is there in having it happen a few years earlier?"

"I will tell you. What was born of them still draws the breath of life; what they built up yet remains; what they loved, taught, and suffered for, lives about us and within us; and should we not allow them to rest in peace?"

"Your warmth shows me that you are thinking of your own grandfather again," replied Lars, "and I must say it seems to me high time the parish should be rid of *him*. He monopolized too much space while he lived; and so it is scarcely worth while to have him lie in the way now that he is dead. Should his corpse prevent a blessing to this parish that would extend through a hundred generations, we may truly say that of all who have been born here, *he* has done us the greatest harm."

Knud Aakre tossed back his disorderly hair, his eyes flashed, his whole person looked like a bent steel spring.

"How much of a blessing what you are speaking about may be, I have already shown. It has the same character as all the other blessings with which you have supplied the parish, namely, a doubtful one. It is true, you have provided us with a new church, but you have also filled it with a new spirit, — and it is not that of love. True, you have furnished us with new roads, but also with new roads to de-

struction, as is now plainly manifest in the mis-
fortunes of many. True, you have diminished
our public taxes, but you have increased our
private ones; lawsuits, promissory notes, and
bankruptcies are no fruitful gifts to a commu-
nity. And *you* dare dishonor in his grave the
man whom the whole parish blesses? You dare
assert that he lies in our way; aye, no doubt
he does lie in your way, this is plain enough
now, for his grave will be the cause of your
downfall! The spirit which has reigned over
you, and until to-day over us all, was not born
to rule but to enter into servitude. The churchyard will surely be allowed to remain in peace;
but to-day it shall have one grave added to
it, namely, that of your popularity which is now
to be buried there."

Lars Högstad rose, white as a sheet; his lips
parted, but he was unable to utter a word, and
the straw fell. After three or four vain efforts
to find it again and recover his powers of speech,
he burst forth like a volcano with, —

"And so these are the thanks I get for all
my toil and drudgery! If such a woman-
preacher is to be allowed to rule — why, then,
may the devil be your chairman if ever I set
my foot here again! I have kept things together until this day, and after me your trash

will fall into a thousand pieces, but let it tumble down now — here is the register!" And he flung it on the table. "Shame on such an assembly of old women and brats!" Here he struck the table with great violence. "Shame on the whole parish that it can see a man rewarded as I am now."

He brought down his fist once more with such force that the great court-house table shook, and the inkstand with its entire contents tumbled to the floor, marking for all future generations the spot where Lars Högstad fell in spite of all his prudence, his long rule, and his patience.

He rushed to the door and in a few moments had left the place. The entire assembly remained motionless; for the might of his voice and of his wrath had frightened them, until Knud Aakre, remembering the taunt he had received at the time of *his* fall, with beaming countenance and imitating Lars's voice, exclaimed : —

"Is *this* to be the decisive blow in the matter?"

The whole assembly burst into peals of merriment at these words! The solemn meeting ended in laughter, talk, and high glee; only a few left the place, those remaining behind

called for drink to add to their food, and a night
of thunder succeeded a day of lightning. Every
one felt as happy and independent as of yore,
ere the commanding spirit of Lars had cowed
their souls into dumb obedience. They drank
toasts to their freedom; they sang, indeed,
finally they danced, Kuud Aakre and the vice-
chairman taking the lead and all the rest following, while boys and girls joined in, and
the young folks outside shouted "Hurrah!" for
such a jollification they had never before seen!

CHAPTER III.

LARS moved about in the large rooms at Högstad, without speaking a word. His wife, who
loved him, but always in fear and trembling,
dared not come into his presence. The man-
agement of the gard and of the house might be
carried on as best it could, while on the other
hand there kept growing a multitude of letters,
which passed back and forth between Högstad
and the parish, and Högstad and the post-office;
for Lars had claims against the parish board,
and these not being satisfied he prosecuted;

against the savings-bank, which were also un-
satisfied, and so resulted in another suit. He
took offense at expressions in the letters he
received and went to law again, now against
the chairman of the parish board, now against
the president of the savings-bank. At the same
time there were dreadful articles in the news-
papers, which report attributed to him, and
which were the cause of great dissension in
the parish, inciting neighbor against neighbor.
Sometimes he was absent whole weeks, no one
knew where, and when he returned he lived as
secluded as before. At church he had not been
seen after the great scene at the representatives' meeting.

Then one Saturday evening the priest brought
tidings that the railroad was to run through
the parish after all, and across the old churchyard! It struck like lightning into every
home. The unanimous opposition of the parish board had been in vain, Lars Högstad's
influence had been stronger. This was the
meaning of his journeys, this was his work!
Involuntary admiration of the man and his
stubborn persistence tended to suppress the
dissatisfaction of the people at their own defeat,
and the more they discussed the matter the
more reconciled they became; for a fact accom-

plished always contains within itself reasons
why it is so, which gradually force themselves
upon us after there is no longer possibility
of change. The people assembled about the
church the next day, and they could not help
laughing as they met one another. And just
as the whole congregation, young and old, men
and women, aye, even children, were all talking
about Lars Högstad, his ability, his rigorous
will, his immense influence, he himself with
his whole household came driving up in four
conveyances, one after the other. It was two
years since his last visit there ! He alighted
and passed through the crowd, while all, as by
one impulse, unhesitatingly greeted him, but he
did not deign to bestow a glance on either side,
nor to return a single salutation. His little
wife, pale as death, followed him. Inside of
the church, the astonishment grew to such a
pitch that as one after another caught sight of
him they stopped singing and only stared at
him. Knud Aakre, who sat in his pew in front
of Lars, noticed that there was something the
matter, and as he perceived nothing remarkable
in front of him, he turned round. He saw Lars
bowed over his hymn-book, searching for the
place.

He had not seen him since that evening at

the meeting, and such a complete change he had not believed possible. For this was no victor! The thin, soft hair was thinner than ever, the face was haggard and emaciated, the eyes hollow and bloodshot, the giant neck had dwindled into wrinkles and cords. Knud comprehended at a glance what this man had gone through; he was seized with a feeling of strong sympathy, indeed, he felt something of the old love stirring within his breast. He prayed for Lars to his God, and made a resolute vow that he would seek him after service; but Lars had started on ahead. Knud resolved to call on him that evening. His wife, however, held him back.

"Lars is one of those," said she, "who can scarcely bear a debt of gratitude: keep away from him until he has an opportunity to do you some favor, and then perhaps he will come to you!"

But he did not come. He appeared now and then at church, but nowhere else, and he associated with no one. On the other hand, he now devoted himself to his gard and other business with the passionate zeal of one who had determined to make amends in one year for the neglect of many; and, indeed, there were those who said that this was imperative.

Railroad operations in the valley began very soon. As the line was to go directly past Lars's gard, he tore down the portion of his house that faced the road, in order to build a large and handsome balcony, for he was determined that his gard should attract attention. This work was just being done when the temporary rails for the conveyance of gravel and timber to the road were laid and a small locomotive was sent to the spot. It was a beautiful autumn evening that the first gravel car was to pass over the road. Lars stood on his front steps, to hear the first signal and to see the first column of smoke; all the people of the gard were gathered about him. He gazed over the parish, illumined by the setting sun, and he felt that he would be remembered as long as a train should come roaring through this fertile valley. A sense of forgiveness glided into his soul. He looked toward the churchyard, a part of which still remained, with crosses bowed down to the ground, but a part of it was now the railroad. He was just endeavoring to define his own feeling when the first signal whistled, and presently the train came slowly working its way along, attended by a cloud of smoke, mingled with sparks, for the locomotive was fed with pine wood. The wind blew toward the house so that those standing without were soon enveloped in a dense smoke, but as this cleared away Lars saw the train working its way down through the valley like a strong will.

He was content, and entered his house like one who has come from a long day's work. The image of his grandfather stood before him at this moment. This grandfather had raised the family from poverty to prosperity ; true, a portion of his honor as a citizen was consumed in the act, but he had advanced nevertheless ! His faults were the prevailing ones of his time : they were based on the uncertain boundary lines of the moral conceptions of his day. Every age has its uncertain moral distinctions and its victims to the endeavor to define them properly.

Honor be to him in his grave, for he had suffered and toiled ! Peace be with him ! It must be good to rest in the end. But he was not allowed to rest because of his grandson's vast ambition ; his ashes were thrown up with the stones and the gravel. Nonsense ! he would only smile that his grandson's work passed over his head.

Amid thoughts like these Lars had undressed and gone to bed. Once more his grandfather' image glided before him. It was sterner now than the first time. Weariness enfeebles us, and Lars began to reproach himself. But he defended himself also. What did his grandfather want? Surely he ought to be satisfied now, for the family honor was proclaimed in loud tones above his grave. Who else had such a monument? And yet what is this? These two monstrous eyes of fire and this hissing, roaring sound belong no longer to the locomotive, for they turn away from the railroad track. And from the churchyard straight toward the house comes an immense procession. The eyes of fire are his grandfather's, and the long line of followers are all the dead. The train advances steadily toward the gard, roaring, crackling, flashing. The windows blaze in the reflection of the dead men's eyes. Lars made a mighty effort to control himself, for this was a dream, unquestionably but a dream. Only wait until I am awake! There, now I am awake. Come on, poor ghosts!

And lo! they really did come from the churchyard, overthrowing road, rails, locomotive and train, so that these fell with a mighty crash to the ground, and the green sod appeared in their stead, dotted with graves and crosses as before. Like mighty champions they advanced, and the hymn, "Let the dead repose in peace!" preceded them. Lars knew it; for through all these years it had been sighing within his soul, and now it had become his requiem; for this was death and death's visions. The cold sweat started out over his whole body, for nearer and nearer — and behold, on the window pane! there they are now, and he heard some one speak his name. Overpowered with dread he struggled to scream; for he was being strangled, a cold hand was clinching his throat and he regained his voice in an agonized: " Help me!" and awoke. The window had been broken in from the outside; the pieces flew all about his head. He sprang up. A man stood at the window, surrounded by smoke and flames.

"The gard is on fire, Lars! We will help you out!"

It was Knud Aakre.

When Lars regained his consciousness, he was lying outside in a bleak wind, which chilled his limbs. There was not a soul with him; he saw the flaming gard to the left; around him his cattle were grazing and making their voices heard; the sheep were huddled together in a frightened flock; the household goods were scattered about, and when he looked again he saw some one sitting on a knoll close by, weeping. It was his wife. He called her by name. She started.

"The Lord Jesus be praised that you are alive!" cried she, coming forward and seating herself, or rather throwing herself down in front of him. "O God! O God! We surely have had enough of this railroad now!"

"The railroad?" asked he, but ere the words had escaped his lips, a clear comprehension of the case passed like a shudder over him; for, of course, sparks from the locomotive that had fallen among the shavings of the new side wall had been the cause of the fire. Lars sat there brooding in silence; his wife, not daring to utter another word, began to search for his clothes; for what she had spread over him, as he lay senseless, had fallen off. He accepted her attentions in silence, but as she knelt before him to cover his feet, he laid his hand on her head. Falling forward she buried her face in his lap and wept aloud. There were many who eyed her curiously. But Lars understood her and said, —

"You are the only friend I have."

Even though it had cost the gard to hear these words, it mattered not to her; she felt so happy that she gained courage, and rising up and looking humbly into her husband's face, she said, —

"Because there is no one else who understands you."

Then a hard heart melted, and tears rolled down the man's cheeks as he clung to his wife's hand.

Now he talked to her as to his own soul. Now too she opened to him her mind. They also talked about how all this had happened, or rather he listened while she told about it. Knud Aakre had been the first to see the fire, had roused his people, sent the girls out over his parish, while he had hastened himself with men and horses to the scene of the conflagration, where all were sleeping. He had engineered the extinguishing of the flames and the rescuing of the household goods, and had himself dragged Lars from the burning room, and carried him to the left side of the house from where the wind was blowing and had laid him out here in the churchyard.

And while they were talking of this, some one came driving rapidly up the road and turned into the churchyard, where he alighted. It was Knud, who had been home after his church-cart, — the one in which they had so many times ridden together to and from the meetings of the parish board. Now he requested Lars to get in and ride home with him. They grasped each other by the hand, the one sitting, the other standing.

" Come with me now," said Knud.

Without a word of reply, Lars rose. Side by side they walked to the cart. Lars was helped in ; Knud sat down beside him. What they talked about as they drove along, or afterwards in the little chamber at Aakre, where they remained together until late in the morning, has never been known. But from that day they were inseparable as before.

As soon as misfortune overtakes a man, every one learns what he is worth. And so the parish undertook to rebuild Lars Högstad's houses, and to make them larger and handsomer than any others in the valley. He was reëlected chairman, but with Knud Aakre at his side ; he never again failed to take counsel of Knud's intelligence and heart — and from that day forth nothing went to ruin.

THROND.

There was once a man named Alf, who had raised great expectations among his fellow-parishioners because he excelled most of them both in the work he accomplished and in the advice he gave. Now when this man was thirty years old, he went to live up the mountain and cleared a piece of land for farming, about fourteen miles from any settlement. Many people wondered how he could endure thus depending on himself for companionship, but they were still more astonished when, a few years later, a young girl from the valley, and one, too, who had been the gayest of the gay at all the social gatherings and dances of the parish, was willing to share his solitude.

This couple were called " the people in the wood," and the man was known by the name " Alf in the wood." People viewed him with inquisitive eyes when they met him at church or at work, because they did not understand him; but neither did he take the trouble to give them any explanation of his conduct. His wife was only seen in the parish twice, and on one of these occasions it was to present a child for baptism.

This child was a son, and he was called Thrond. When he grew larger his parents often talked about needing help, and as they could not afford to take a full-grown servant, they hired what they called "a half:" they brought into their house a girl of fourteen, who took care of the boy while the father and mother were busy in the field.

This girl was not the brightest person in the world, and the boy soon observed that his mother's words were easy to comprehend, but that it was hard to get at the meaning of what Ragnhild said. He never talked much with his father, and he was rather afraid of him, for the house had to be kept very quiet when he was at home.

One Christmas Eve — they were burning two candles on the table, and the father was drinking from a white flask — the father took the boy up in his arms and set him on his lap, looked him sternly in the eyes and exclaimed, —

"Ugh, boy!" Then he added more gently:

" Why, you are not so much afraid. Would you have the courage to listen to a story ? "

The boy made no reply, but he looked full in his father's face. His father then told him about a man from Vaage, whose name was Blessom. This man was in Copenhagen for the purpose of getting the king's verdict in a law-suit he was engaged in, and he was detained so long that Christmas Eve overtook him there. Blessom was greatly annoyed at this, and as he was sauntering about the streets fancying himself at home, he saw a very large man, in a white, short coat, walking in front of him.

" How fast you are walking ! " said Blessom.

" I have a long distance to go in order to get home this evening," replied the man.

" Where are you going ? "

" To Vaage," answered the man, and walked on.

" Why, that is very nice," said Blessom, " for that is where I was going, too."

" Well, then, you may ride with me, if you will stand on the runners of my sledge," an swered the man, and turned into a side street where his horse was standing.

He mounted his seat and looked over his shoulder at Blessom, who was just getting on the runners.

"You had better hold fast," said the stranger.

Blossom did as he was told, and it was well he did, for their journey was evidently not by land.

"It seems to me that you are driving on the water," cried Blossom.

"I am," said the man, and the spray whirled about them.

But after a while it seemed to Blossom their course no longer lay on the water.

"It seems to me we are moving through the air," said he.

"Yes, so we are," replied the stranger.

But when they had gone still farther, Blossom thought he recognized the parish they were driving through.

"Is not this Vaage?" cried he.

"Yes, now we are there," replied the stranger, and it seemed to Blossom that they had gone pretty fast.

"Thank you for the good ride," said he.

"Thanks to yourself," replied the man, and added, as he whipped up his horse, "Now you had better not look after me."

"No, indeed," thought Blossom, and started over the hills for home.

But just then so loud and terrible a crash

was heard behind him that it seemed as if the whole mountain must be tumbling down, and a bright light was shed over the surrounding landscape; he looked round and beheld the stranger in the white coat driving through the crackling flames into the open mountain, which was yawning wide to receive him, like some huge gate. Blessom felt somewhat strange in regard to his traveling companion; and thought he would look in another direction; but as he had turned his head so it remained, and never more could Blessom get it straight again.

The boy had never heard anything to equal this in all his life. He dared not ask his father for more, but early the next morning he asked his mother if she knew any stories. Yes, of course she did; but hers were chiefly about princesses who were in captivity for seven years, until the right prince came along. The boy believed that everything he heard or read about took place close around him.

He was about eight years old when the first stranger entered their door one winter evening. He had black hair, and this was something Thrond had never seen before. The stranger saluted them with a short "Good-evening!" and came forward. Thrond grew frightened and sat down on a cricket by the hearth. The mother asked the man to take a seat on the bench along the wall; he did so, and then the mother could examine his face more closely.

"Dear me! is not this Knud the fiddler?" cried she.

"Yes, to be sure it is. It has been a long time since I played at your wedding."

"Oh, yes; it is quite a while now. Have you been on a long journey?"

"I have been playing for Christmas, on the other side of the mountain. But half way down the slope I began to feel very badly, and I was obliged to come in here to rest."

The mother brought forward food for him; he sat down to the table, but did not say "in the name of Jesus," as the boy had been accustomed to hear. When he had finished eating, he got up from the table, and said, —

"Now I feel very comfortable; let me rest a little while."

And he was allowed to rest on Thrond's bed.

For Thrond a bed was made on the floor. As the boy lay there, he felt cold on the side that was turned away from the fire, and that was the left side. He discovered that it was because this side was exposed to the chill night air; for he was lying out in the wood. How came he in the wood? He got up and looked

about him, and saw that there was fire burning
a long distance off, and that he was actually
alone in the wood. He longed to go home to
the fire; but could not stir from the spot.
Then a great fear overcame him; for wild
beasts might be roaming about, trolls and ghosts
might appear to him; he must get home to the
fire; but he could not stir from the spot. Then
his terror grew, he strove with all his might to
gain self-control, and was at last able to cry,
"Mother," and then he awoke.

"Dear child, you have had bad dreams,"
said she, and took him up.

A shudder ran through him, and he glanced
round. The stranger was gone, and he dared
not inquire after him.

His mother appeared in her black dress, and
started for the parish. She came home with
two new strangers, who also had black hair
and who wore flat caps. They did not say "in
the name of Jesus," when they ate, and they
talked in low tones with the father. Afterward the latter and they went into the barn,
and came out again with a large box, which
the men carried between them. They placed it
on a sled, and said farewell. Then the mother
said: —

"Wait a little, and take with you the smaller
box he brought here with him."

And she went in to get it. But one of the men said, —

"*He* can have that," and he pointed at Thrond.

"Use it as well as *he* who is now lying *here*," added the other stranger, pointing at the large box.

Then they both laughed and went on. Thrond looked at the little box which thus came into his possession.

"What is there in it?" asked he.

"Carry it in and find out," said the mother.

He did as he was told, but his mother helped him open it. Then a great joy lighted up his face; for he saw something very light and fine lying there.

"Take it up," said his mother.

He put just one finger down on it, but quickly drew it back again, in great alarm.

"It cries," said he.

"Have courage," said his mother, and he grasped it with his whole hand and drew it forth from the box.

He weighed it and turned it round, he laughed and felt of it.

"Dear me! what is it?" asked he, for it was as light as a toy.

"It is a fiddle."

This was the way that Thrond Alfson got his first violin.

The father could play a little, and he taught the boy how to handle the instrument; the mother could sing the tunes she remembered from her dancing days, and these the boy learned, but soon began to make new ones for himself. He played all the time he was not at his books; he played until his father once told him he was fading away before his eyes. All the boy had read and heard until that time was put into the fiddle. The tender, delicate string was his mother; the one that lay close beside it, and always accompanied his mother, was Ragnhild. The coarse string, which he seldom ventured to play on, was his father. But of the last solemn string he was half afraid, and he gave no name to it. When he played a wrong note on the E string, it was the cat; but when he took a wrong note on his father's string, it was the ox. The bow was Blessom, who drove from Copenhagen to Vaage in one night. And every tune he played represented something. The one containing the long solemn tones was his mother in her black dress. The one that jerked and skipped was like Moses, who stuttered and smote the rock with his staff. The one that had to be played quietly, with the bow moving lightly over the strings, was the hulder in yonder fog, calling together her cattle, where no one but herself could see.

But the music wafted him onward over the mountains, and a great yearning took possession of his soul. One day when his father told about a little boy who had been playing at the fair and who had earned a great deal of money, Thrond waited for his mother in the kitchen and asked her softly if he could not go to the fair and play for people.

"Who ever heard of such a thing!" said his mother; but she immediately spoke to his father about it.

"He will get out into the world soon enough," answered the father; and he spoke in such a way that the mother did not ask again.

Shortly after this, the father and mother were talking at table about some new settlers who had recently moved up on the mountain and were about to be married. They had no fiddler for the wedding, the father said.

"Could not I be the fiddler?" whispered the boy, when he was alone in the kitchen once more with his mother.

"What, a little boy like you?" said she; but she went out to the barn where his father was and told him about it.

"He has never been in the parish," she added, "he has never seen a church."

"I should not think you would ask about such things," said Alf; but neither did he say anything more, and so the mother thought she had permission. Consequently she went over to the new settlers and offered the boy's services.

"The way he plays," said she, "no little boy has ever played before;" and the boy was to be allowed to come.

What joy there was at home! Thrond played from morning until evening and practiced new tunes; at night he dreamed about them: they bore him far over the hills, away to foreign lands, as though he were afloat on sailing clouds. His mother made a new suit of clothes for him; but his father would not take part in what was going on.

The last night he did not sleep, but thought out a new tune about the church which he had never seen. He was up early in the morning, and so was his mother, in order to get him his breakfast, but he could not eat. He put on his new clothes and took his fiddle in his hand, and it seemed to him as though a bright light were glowing before his eyes. His mother accompanied him out on the flag-stone, and stood watching him as he ascended the slopes; — it was the first time he had left home.

His father got quietly out of bed and walked to the window; he stood there following the boy with his eyes until he heard the mother out on the flag-stone, then he went back to bed and was lying down when she came in.

She kept stirring about him, as if she wanted to relieve her mind of something. And finally it came out: —

"I really think I must walk down to the church and see how things are going."

He made no reply, and therefore she considered the matter settled, dressed herself and started.

It was a glorious, sunny day, the boy walked rapidly onward; he listened to the song of the birds and saw the sun glittering among the foliage, while he proceeded on his way, with his fiddle under his arm. And when he reached the bride's house, he was still so occupied with his own thoughts, that he observed neither the bridal splendor nor the procession; he merely asked if they were about to start, and learned that they were. He walked on in advance with his fiddle, and he played the whole morning into it, and the tones he produced resounded through the trees.

" Will we soon see the church ? " he asked over his shoulder.

For a long time he received only " No " for an answer, but at last some one said:

" As soon as you reach that crag yonder, you will see it."

He threw his newest tune into the fiddle, the bow danced on the strings, and he kept his eyes fixed intently before him. There lay the parish right in front of him !

The first thing he saw was a little light mist, curling like smoke on the opposite mountain side. His eyes wandered over the green meadow and the large houses, with windows which glistened beneath the scorching rays of the sun, like the glacier on a winter's day. The houses kept increasing in size, the windows in number, and here on one side of him lay the enormous red house, in front of which horses were tied; little children were playing on a hill, dogs were sitting watching them. But everywhere there penetrated a long, heavy tone, that shook him from head to foot, and everything he saw seemed to vibrate with that tone. Then suddenly he saw a large, straight house, with a tall, glittering staff reaching up to the skies. And below, a hundred windows blazed, so that the house seemed to be enveloped in flames.

This must be the church, the boy thought, and the music must come from it! Round about stood a vast multitude of people, and they all looked alike! He put them forthwith into relations with the church, and thus acquired a respect mingled with awe for the smallest child he saw.

"Now I must play," thought Thrond, and tried to do so.

But what was this? The fiddle had no longer any sound in it. There must be some defect in the strings; he examined, but could find none.

"Then it must be because I do not press on hard enough, and he drew his bow with a firmer hand; but the fiddle seemed as if it were cracked.

He changed the tune that was meant to represent the church into another, but with equally bad results; no music was produced, only squeaking and wailing. He felt the cold sweat start out over his face, he thought of all these wise people who were standing here and perhaps laughing him to scorn, this boy who at home could play so beautifully but who here failed to bring out a single tone!

"Thank God that mother is not here to see my shame!" said he softly to himself, as he played among the people; but lo! there she stood, in her black dress, and she shrank farther and farther away.

At that moment he beheld far up on the spire, the black-haired man who had given him the fiddle. "Give it back to me," he now shouted, laughing and stretching out his arms, and the spire went up and down with him, up and down. But the boy took the fiddle under one arm, screaming, "You shall not have it!" and turning, ran away from the people, beyond the houses, onward through meadow and field, until his strength forsook him, and then sank to the ground.

There he lay for a long time, with his face toward the earth, and when finally he looked round he saw and heard only God's infinite blue sky that floated above him, with its ever-lasting sough. This was so terrible to him that he had to turn his face to the ground again. When he raised his head once more his eyes fell on his fiddle, which lay at his side.

"This is all your fault!" shouted the boy, and seized the instrument with the intention of dashing it to pieces, but hesitated as he looked at it.

"We have had many a happy hour together,' said he, then paused. Presently he said: "The strings must be severed, for they are worthless." And he took out a knife and cut. "Oh!" cried the E string, in a short, pained tone. The boy cut. "Oh!" wailed the next; but the boy cut. "Oh!" said the third, mournfully; and he paused at the fourth. A sharp pain seized him; that fourth string, to which he never dared give a name, he did not cut. Now a feeling came over him that it was not the fault of the strings that he was unable to play, and just then he saw his mother walking slowly up the slope toward where he was lying, that she might take him home with her. A greater fright than ever overcame him; he held the fiddle by the severed strings, sprang to his feet, and shouted down to her, —

"No, mother! I will not go home again until I can play what I have seen to-day."

A DANGEROUS WOOING.

WHEN Aslaug had become a grown-up girl, there was not much peace to be had at Huseby; for there the finest boys in the parish quarreled and fought night after night. It was worst of all on Saturday nights; but then old Knud Huseby never went to bed without keeping his leather breeches on, nor without having a birch stick by his bedside.

"If I have a daughter, I shall look after her, too," said old Huseby.

Thore Næset was only a houseman's son; nevertheless there were those who said that he was the one who came oftenest to see the gardman's daughter at Huseby. Old Knud did not like this, and declared also that it was not true, "for he had never seen him there." But people smiled slyly among themselves, and thought that had he searched in the corners of the room instead of fighting with all those who were making a noise and uproar in the middle of the floor, he would have found Thore.

Spring came and Aslaug went to the sæter with the cattle. Then, when the day was warm down in the valley, and the mountain rose cool above the haze, and when the bells tinkled, the shepherd dog barked, and Aslaug sang and blew the loor on the mountain side, then the hearts of the young fellows who were at work down on the meadow would ache, and the first Saturday night they all started up to the mountain sæter, one faster than the other. But still more rapidly did they come down again, for behind the door at the sæter there stood one who received each of them as he came, and gave him so sound a whipping that he forever afterward remembered the threat that followed it, —

"Come again another time and you shall have some more."

According to what these young fellows knew, there was only one in the parish who could use his fists in this way, and that was Thore Næset. And these rich gardmen's sons thought it was a shame that this houseman's son should cut them all out at the Huseby sæter.

So thought, also, old Knud, when the matter reached his ears, and said, moreover, that if there was nobody else who could tackle Thore, then he and his sons would try it. Knud, it is true, was growing old, but although he was nearly sixty, he would at times have a wrestle or two with his eldest son, when it was too dull for him at some party or other.

Up to the Huseby sæter there was but one road, and that led straight through the gard. The next Saturday evening, as Thore was going to the sæter, and was stealing on his tiptoes across the yard, a man rushed right at his breast as he came near the barn.

"What do you want of me?" said Thore, and knocked his assailant flat on the ground.

"That you shall soon find out," said another fellow from behind, giving Thore a blow on the back of the head. This was the brother of the former assailant.

"Here comes the third," said old Knud, rushing forward to join the fray.

The danger made Thore stronger. He was as limber as a willow and his blows left their marks. He dodged from one side to the other. Where the blows fell he was not, and where his opponents least expected blows from him, they got them. He was, however, at last completely beaten; but old Knud frequently said afterwards that a stouter fellow he had scarcely ever tackled. The fight was continued until blood flowed, but then Huseby cried, —

" Stop ! " and added, " If you can manage to get by the Huseby wolf and his cubs next Saturday night, the girl shall be yours."

Thore dragged himself homeward as best he could ; and as soon as he got home he went to bed.

At Huseby there was much talk about the fight ; but everybody said, —

" What did he want there ? "

There was one, however, who did not say so, and that was Aslaug. She had expected Thore that Saturday night, and when she heard what had taken place between him and her father, she sat down and had a good cry, saying to herself, —

" If I cannot have Thore, there will never be another happy day for me in this world."

Thore had to keep his bed all day Sunday ; and Monday, too, he felt that he must do the same. Tuesday came, and it was such a beautiful day. It had rained during the night. The mountain was wet and green. The fragrance of the leaves was wafted in through the open window ; down the mountain sides came the sound of the cow-bells, and some one was heard singing up in the glen. Had it not been for his mother, who was sitting in the room, Thore would have wept from impatient vexation.

Wednesday came and still Thore was in bed;
but on Thursday he began to wonder whether
he could not get well by Saturday; and on Fri-
day he rose. He remembered well the words
Aslaug's father had spoken: "If you can manage to get by the Huseby wolf and his cubs
next Saturday, the girl shall be yours." He
looked over toward the Huseby sæter again and
again. "I cannot get more than another
thrashing," thought Thore.

Up to the Huseby sæter there was but one
road, as before stated; but a clever fellow might
manage to get there, even if he did not take
the beaten track. If he rowed out on the fjord
below, and past the little tongue of land yonder, and thus reached the other side of the
mountain, he might contrive to climb it, though
it was so steep that a goat could scarcely venture there — and a goat is not very apt to be
timid in climbing the mountains, you know.

Saturday came, and Thore stayed without
doors all day long. The sunlight played upon
the foliage, and every now and then an allur-
ing song was heard from the mountains. As
evening drew near, and the mist was stealing
up the slope, he was still sitting outside of the
door. He looked up the mountain, and all was
still. He looked over toward the Huseby gard.

Then he pushed out his boat and rowed round the point of land.

Up at the sæter sat Aslaug, through with her day's work. She was thinking that Thore would not come this evening, but that there would come all the more in his stead. Presently she let loose the dog, but told no one whither she was going. She seated herself where she could look down into the valley; but a dense fog was rising, and, moreover, she felt little disposed to look down that way, for everything reminded her of what had occurred. So she moved, and without thinking what she was doing, she happened to go over to the other side of the mountain, and there she sat down and gazed out over the sea. There was so much peace in this far-reaching sea-view!

Then she felt like singing. She chose a song with long notes, and the music sounded far into the still night. She felt gladdened by it, and so she sang another verse. But then it seemed to her as if some one answered her from the glen far below. "Dear me, what can that be?" thought Aslaug. She went forward to the brink of the precipice, and threw her arms around a slender birch, which hung trembling over the steep. She looked down but saw nothing. The fjord lay silent and calm. Not

even a bird ruffled its smooth surface. Aslaug
sat down and began singing again. Then she
was sure that some one responded with the
same tune and nearer than the first time. " It
must be somebody, after all." Aslaug sprang
up and bent out over the brink of the steep;
and there, down at the foot of a rocky wall,
she saw a boat moored, and it was so far down
that it appeared like a tiny shell. She looked
a little farther up, and her eyes fell on a red
cap, and under the cap she saw a young man,
who was working his way up the almost per-
pendicular side of the mountain. " Dear me,
who can that be ? " asked Aslaug, as she let go
of the birch and sprang far back.

She dared not answer her own question, for
she knew very well who it was. She threw
herself down on the greensward and took hold
of the grass with both hands, as though it were
she who must not let go her hold. But the
grass came up by the roots.

She cried aloud and prayed God to help
Thore. But then it struck her that this conduct of Thore's was really tempting God, and
therefore no help could be expected.

" Just this once ! " she implored.

And she threw her arms around the dog, as
if it were Thore she were keeping from loosing

his hold. She rolled over the grass with him, and the moments seemed years. But then the dog tore himself away. "Bow-bow," he barked over the brink of the steep and wagged his tail. "Bow-wow," he barked at Aslaug, and threw his forepaws up on her. "Bow-wow," over the precipice again; and a red cap appeared over the brow of the mountain and Thore lay in her arms.

Now when old Knud Huseby heard of this, he made a very sensible remark, for he said, —

"That boy is worth having; the girl shall be his."

THE BEAR HUNTER.

———◆———

A WORSE boy to tell lies than the priest's oldest son could scarcely be found in the whole parish; he was also a very good reader; there was no lack on that score, and what he read the peasants were glad to hear, but when it was something they were well pleased with, he would make up more of the same kind, as much as he thought they wanted. His own stories were mostly about strong men and about love.

Soon the priest noticed that the threshing up in the barn was being done in a more and more lazy manner; he went to see what the matter was, and behold it was Thorvald, who stood there telling stories. Soon the quantity of wood brought home from the forest became wonderfully small; he went to see what the trouble was, and there stood Thorvald again, telling stories. There must be an end to this, thought the priest; and he sent the boy to the nearest school.

Only peasant children attended this school, but the priest thought it would be too expensive to keep a private tutor for this one boy. But Thorvald had not been a week among the scholars, before one of his schoolmates came in pale as a corpse, and said he had met some of the underground folk coming along the road. Another boy, still paler, followed, and said that he had actually seen a man without a head walking about and moving the boats down by the landing-place. And what was worst of all, little Knud Pladsen and his young sister, one evening, as they were returning home from school, came running back, almost out of their senses, crying, and declaring that they had heard the bear up near the parsonage; nay, little Marit had even seen his gray eyes sparkle. But now the school-master got terribly angry, struck the table with his ferule, and asked what the deuce — God pardon me my wicked sin — had gotten into the school-children.

" One is growing more crazy than the other," said he. " There lurks a hulder in every bush; there sits a merman under every boat; the bear is out in midwinter! Have you no more faith in your God or in your catechism," quoth he, " or do you believe in all kinds of deviltry, and in all the terrible powers of darkness, and in bears roaming about in the middle of winter?"

But then he calmed down somewhat after a while, and asked little Marit whether she really did not dare to go home. The child sobbed and cried, and declared that it was utterly impossible. The school-master then said that Thorvald, who was the eldest of those remaining, should go with her through the wood.

"No, he has seen the bear himself," cried Marit; " it was he who told us about it."

Thorvald shrank within himself, where he was sitting, especially when the school-master looked at him and drew the ferule affectionately through his left hand.

" Have you seen the bear?" he asked, quietly.

" Well, at any rate, I know," said Thorvald, " that our overseer found a bear's den up in the priest's wood, the day he was out ptarmigan shooting."

" But have you seen the bear yourself? "

" It was not one, it was two large ones, and perhaps there were two smaller ones besides, as the old ones generally have their last year's cubs and this year's, too, with them."

" But have *you* seen them?" reiterated the school-master, still more mildly, as he kept drawing the ferule between his fingers.

Thorvald was silent for a moment.

" I saw the bear that Lars, the hunter, felled last year, at any rate."

Then the school-master came a step nearer, and asked, so pleasantly that the boy became frightened, —

" Have you seen the bears up in the parsonage wood, I ask ? "

Thorvald did not say another word.

" Perhaps your memory did not serve you quite right this time ? " said the school-master, taking the boy by the jacket collar and striking his own side with the ferule.

Thorvald did not say a word; the other children dared not look that way. Then the school-master said earnestly, —

" It is wicked for a priest's son to tell lies, and still more wicked to teach the poor peasant children to do such things."

And so the boy escaped for that time.

But the next day at school (the teacher had been called up to the priest's and the children were left to themselves) Marit was the first one to ask Thorvald to tell her something about the bear again.

" But you get so frightened," said he.

" Oh, I think I will have to stand it," said she, and moved closer to her brother.

" Ah, now you had better believe it will be shot!" said Thorvald, and nodded his head. " There has come a fellow to the parish who is able to shoot it. No sooner had Lars, the hunter, heard about the bear's den up in the parsonage wood, than he came running through seven whole parishes with a rifle as heavy as the upper mill-stone, and as long as from here to Hans Volden, who sits yonder."

" Mercy!" cried all the children.

" As long?" repeated Thorvald; " yes, it is certainly as long as from here to yonder bench."

" Have you seen it?" asked Ole Böen.

" Have I seen it, do you say? Why, I have been helping to clean it, and that is what Lars will not allow everybody to do, let me tell you. Of course *I* could not lift it, but that made no difference; I only cleaned the lock, and that is not the easiest work, I can tell you."

" People say that gun of Lars's has taken to missing its mark of late," said Hans Volden, leaning back, with both his feet on the desk. ' Ever since that time when Lars shot, up at Osmark, at a bear that was asleep, it misses fire twice and misses the mark the third time."

" Yes, ever since he shot at a bear that was asleep," chimed in the girls.

" The fool ! " added the boys.

" There is only one way in which this diffi-culty with the rifle can be remedied," said Ole Böen, " and that is to thrust a living snake down its barrel."

" Yes, we all know that," said the girls. They wanted to hear something new.

" It is now winter, and snakes are not to be found, and so Lars cannot depend very much upon his rifle," said Hans Volden, thought-fully.

" He wants Niels Böen along with him, does he not ? " asked Thorvald.

" Yes," said the boy from Böen's, who was, of course, best posted in regard to this ; " but Niels will get permission neither from his mother nor from his sister. His father cer-tainly died from the wrestle he had with the bear up at the sæter last year, and now they have no one but Niels."

" Is it so dangerous, then ? " asked a little boy.

" Dangerous ? " cried Thorvald. " The bear has as much sense as ten men, and as much strength as twelve."

" Yes, we know that," said the girls once more. They were bent on hearing something new.

"But Niels is like his father; I dare say he will go along," continued Thorvald.

"Of course he will go along," said Ole Böen; "this morning early, before any one was stirring over yonder at our gard, I saw Niels Böen, Lars the hunter, and one man more, going up the mountain with their rifles. I should not be surprised if they were going to the parsonage wood."

"Was it early?" asked the children, in concert.

"Very early! I was up before mother, and started the fire."

"Did Lars have the long rifle?" asked Hans.

"That I do not know, but the one he had was as long as from here to the chair."

"Oh, what a story!" said Thorvald.

"Why, you said so yourself," answered Ole.

"No, the long rifle which I saw, he will scarcely use any more."

"Well, this one was, at all events, as long — as long — as from here, nearly over to the chair."

"Ah! perhaps he had it with him then after all."

"Just think," said Marit, "now they are up among the bears."

"And at this very moment they may be in a fight," said Thorvald.

Then followed a deep, nay, almost solemn silence.

"I think I will go," said Thorvald, taking his cap.

"Yes! yes! then you will find out something," shouted all the rest, and they became full of life again.

"But the school-master?" said he, and stopped.

"Nonsense! you are the priest's son," said Ole Böen.

"Yes, if the school-master touches me with a finger!" said Thorvald, with a significant nod, in the midst of the deep silence of the rest.

"Will you hit him back?" asked they, eagerly.

"Who knows?" said Thorvald, nodding, and went away.

They thought it best to study while he was gone, but none of them were able to do so, — they had to keep talking about the bear. They began guessing how the affair would turn out. Hans bet with Ole that Lars's rifle had missed fire, and that the bear had sprung at him. Little Knud Pladsen thought they had all fared badly, and the girls took his side. But there came Thorvald.

" Let us go," said he, as he pulled open the door, so excited that he could scarcely speak.

" But the school-master?" asked some of the children.

" The deuce take the school-master! The bear! The bear!" cried Thorvald, and could say no more.

" Is it shot?" asked one, very softly, and the others dared not draw their breath.

Thorvald sat panting for a while, finally he got up, mounted one of the benches, swung his cap, and shouted, —

" Let us go, I say. I will take all the responsibility."

" But where shall we go?" asked Hans.

" The largest bear has been borne down, the others still remain. Niels Böen has been badly hurt, because Lars's rifle missed its mark, and the bears rushed straight at them. The boy who went with them saved himself only by throwing himself flat on the ground, and pretending to be dead, and the bear did not touch him. As soon as Lars and Niels had killed their bear, they shot his also. Hurrah!"

" Hurrah!" shouted all, both girls and boys, and up from their seats, and out through the door, they sprang, and off they ran over field and wood to Böen, as though there was no such thing as a school-master in the whole world.

The girls soon complained that they were not able to keep up, but the boys took them by the hand and away they all rushed.

"Take care not to touch it!" said Thorvald; "it sometimes happens that the bears become alive again."

"Is that so?" asked Marit.

"Yes, and they appear in a new form, so have a care!"

And they kept running.

"Lars shot the largest one ten times before it fell," he began again.

"Just think! ten times!"

And they kept running.

"And Niels stabbed it eighteen times with his knife before it fell!"

"Mercy! what a bear!"

And the children ran so that the sweat poured down from their faces.

Finally they reached the place. Ole Böen pushed the door open and got in first.

"Have a care!" cried Hans after him.

Marit and a little girl that Thorvald and Hans had led between them, were the next ones, and then came Thorvald, who did not go far forward, but remained standing where he could observe the whole scene.

"See the blood!" said he to Hans.

The others hardly knew whether they should venture in just yet.

"Do you see it?" asked a girl of a boy, who stood by her side in the door.

Yes, it is as large as the captain's large horse," answered he, and went on talking to her. It was bound with iron chains, he said, and had even broken the one that had been put about its fore-legs. He could see distinctly that it was alive, and the blood was flowing from it like a waterfall.

Of course, this was not true; but they forgot that when they caught sight of the bear, the rifle, and Niels, who sat there with bandaged wounds after the fight with the bear, and when they heard old Lars the hunter tell how all had happened. So eagerly, and with so much interest did they look and listen, that they did not observe that some one came behind them who also began to tell his story, and that in the following manner: —

"I will teach you to leave the school without my permission, that I will!"

A cry of fright arose from the whole crowd, and out through the door, through the veranda, and out into the yard they ran. Soon they appeared like a lot of black balls, rolling one by one, over the snow-white field, and when the school-master on his old legs followed them to the school-house, he could hear the children reading from afar off; they read until the walls fairly rattled.

Aye, that was a glorious day, the day when the bear-hunter came home! It began in sun-shine and ended in rain, but such days are usuallv the best growing days.

THE FATHER.

———◆———

THE man whose story is here to be told was the wealthiest and most influential person in his parish; his name was Thord Överaas. He appeared in the priest's study one day, tall and earnest.

"I have gotten a son," said he, "and I wish to present him for baptism."

"What shall his name be?"

"Finn, — after my father."

"And the sponsors?"

They were mentioned, and proved to be the best men and women of Thord's relations in the parish.

"Is there anything else?" inquired the priest, and looked up.

The peasant hesitated a little.

"I should like very much to have him baptized by himself," said he, finally.

"That is to say on a week-day?"

"Next Saturday, at twelve o'clock noon."

" Is there anything else?" inquired the priest.

" There is nothing else;" and the peasant twirled his cap, as though he were about to go.

Then the priest rose. " There is yet this, however," said he, and walking toward Thord, he took him by the hand and looked gravely into his eyes: " God grant that the child may become a blessing to you!"

One day sixteen years later, Thord stood once more in the priest's study.

" Really, you carry your age astonishingly well, Thord," said the priest; for he saw no change whatever in the man.

" That is because I have no troubles," replied Thord.

To this the priest said nothing, but after a while he asked: " What is your pleasure this evening?"

" I have come this evening about that son of mine who is to be confirmed to-morrow."

" He is a bright boy."

" I did not wish to pay the priest until I heard what number the boy would have when he takes his place in church to-morrow."

" He will stand number one."

" So I have heard; and here are ten dollars for the priest."

" Is there anything else I can do for you ? "
inquired the priest, fixing his eyes on Thord.

" There is nothing else."

Thord went out.

Eight years more rolled by, and then one
day a noise was heard outside of the priest's
study, for many men were approaching, and at
their head was Thord, who entered first.

The priest looked up and recognized him.

" You come well attended this evening,
Thord," said he.

" I am here to request that the bans may be
published for my son : he is about to marry
Karen Storliden, daughter of Gudmund, who
stands here beside me."

" Why, that is the richest girl in the parish."

" So they say," replied the peasant, stroking
back his hair with one hand.

The priest sat a while as if in deep thought,
then entered the names in his book, without
making any comments, and the men wrote their
signatures underneath.   Thord laid three dollars on the table.

" One is all I am to have," said the priest.

" I know that very well ; but he is my only
child , I want to do it handsomely."

The priest took the money

"This is now the third time, Thord, that you have come here on your son's account."

"But now I am through with him," said Thord, and folding up his pocket-book he said farewell and walked away.

The men slowly followed him.

A fortnight later, the father and son were rowing across the lake, one calm, still day, to Storliden to make arrangements for the wedding.

"This thwart is not secure," said the son, and stood up to straighten the seat on which he was sitting.

At the same moment the board he was standing on slipped from under him; he threw out his arms, uttered a shriek, and fell overboard.

"Take hold of the oar!" shouted the father, springing to his feet and holding out the oar.

But when the son had made a couple of efforts he grew stiff.

"Wait a moment!" cried the father, and began to row toward his son.

Then the son rolled over on his back, gave his father one long look, and sank.

Thord could scarcely believe it; he held the boat still, and stared at the spot where his son had gone down, as though he must surely come to the surface again. There rose some bubbles, then some more, and finally one large one that burst; and the lake lay there as smooth and bright as a mirror again.

For three days and three nights people saw the father rowing round and round the spot, without taking either food or sleep; he was dragging the lake for the body of his son. And toward morning of the third day he found it, and carried it in his arms up over the hills to his gard.

It might have been about a year from that day, when the priest, late one autumn evening, heard some one in the passage outside of the door, carefully trying to find the latch. The priest opened the door, and in walked a tall, thin man, with bowed form and white hair. The priest looked long at him before he recognized him. It was Thord.

"Are you out walking so late?" said the priest, and stood still in front of him.

"Ah, yes! it is late," said Thord, and took a seat.

The priest sat down also, as though waiting. A long, long silence followed. At last Thord said, —

"I have something with me that I should like to give to the poor; I want it to be invested as a legacy in my son's name."

He rose, laid some money on the table, and sat down again. The priest counted it.

"It is a great deal of money," said he.

"It is half the price of my gard. I sold it to-day."

The priest sat long in silence. At last he asked, but gently, —

"What do you propose to do now, Thord?"

"Something better."

They sat there for a while, Thord with downcast eyes, the priest with his eyes fixed on Thord. Presently the priest said, slowly and softly, —

"I think your son has at last brought you a true blessing."

"Yes, I think so myself," said Thord, looking up, while two big tears coursed slowly down his cheeks.

19

THE EAGLE'S NEST.

THE Endregards was the name of a small solitary parish, surrounded by lofty mountains. It lay in a flat and fertile valley, and was intersected by a broad river that flowed down from the mountains. This river emptied into a lake, which was situated close by the parish, and presented a fine view of the surrounding country.

Up the Endre-Lake the man had come rowing, who had first cleared this valley; his name was Endre, and it was his descendants who dwelt here. Some said he had fled hither on account of a murder he had committed, and that was why his family were so dark; others said this was on account of the mountains, which shut out the sun at five o'clock of a midsummer afternoon.

Over this parish there hung an eagle's nest. It was built on a cliff far up the mountains; all could see the mother eagle alight in her nest, but no one could reach it. The male eagle went sailing over the parish, now swooping down after a lamb, now after a kid; once he had also taken a little child and borne it away; therefore there was no safety in the parish as long as the eagle had a nest in this mountain. There was a tradition among the people, that in old times there were two brothers who had climbed up to the nest and torn it down; but nowadays there was no one who was able to reach it.

Whenever two met at the Endregards, they talked about the eagle's nest, and looked up. Every one knew, when the eagles reappeared in the new year, where they had swooped down and done mischief, and who had last endeavored to reach the nest. The youth of the place, from early boyhood, practiced climbing mountains and trees, wrestling and scuffling, in order that one day they might reach the cliff and demolish the nest, as those two brothers had done.

At the time of which this story tells, the best boy at the Endregards was named Leif, and he was not of the Endre family. He had curly hair and small eyes, was clever in all play, and was fond of the fair sex. He early said of himself, that one day he would reach the eagle's nest; but old people remarked that he should not have said so aloud.

This annoyed him, and even before he had reached his prime he made the ascent. It was one bright Sunday forenoon, early in the summer; the young eagles must be just about hatched. A vast multitude of people had gathered together at the foot of the mountain to behold the feat; the old people advising him against attempting it, the young ones urging him on.

But he hearkened only to his own desires, and waiting until the mother eagle left her nest, he gave one spring into the air, and hung in a tree several yards from the ground. The tree grew in a cleft in the rock, and from this cleft he began to climb upward. Small stones loosened under his feet, earth and gravel came rolling down, otherwise all was still, save for the stream flowing behind, with its suppressed, ceaseless murmur. Soon he had reached a point where the mountain began to project; here he hung long by one hand, while his foot groped for a sure resting-place, for he could not see. Many, especially women, turned away, saying he would never have done this had he had parents living. He found footing at last, however sought again, now with the hand, now with the foot, failed, slipped, then hung fast again. They who stood below could hear one another breathing.

Suddenly there rose to her feet, a tall, young girl, who had been sitting on a stone apart from the rest; it was said that she had been betrothed to Leif from early childhood, although he was not of her kindred. Stretching out her arms she called aloud : "Leif, Leif, why do you do this?" Every eye was turned on her. Her father, who was standing close by, gave her a stern look, but she heeded him not. "Come down again, Leif," she cried; "I love you, and there is nothing to be gained up there!"

They could see that he was considering; he hesitated a moment or two, and then started onward. For a long time all went well, for he was sure-footed and had a strong grip; but after a while it seemed as if he were growing weary, for he often paused. Presently a little stone came rolling down as a harbinger, and every one who stood there had to watch its course to the bottom. Some could endure it no longer, and went away. The girl alone still stood on the stone, and wringing her hands continued to gaze upward.

Once more Leif took hold with one hand

but it slipped; she saw this distinctly; then he tried the other; it slipped also. "Leif!" she shouted, so loud that her voice rang through the mountains, and all the others chimed in with her. "He is slipping!" they cried, and stretched up their hands to him, both men and women. He was indeed slipping, carrying with him sand, stones, and earth; slipping, continually slipping, ever faster and faster. The people turned away, and then they heard a rustling and scraping in the mountain behind them, after which, something fell with a heavy thud, like a great piece of wet earth.

When they could look round again, he was lying there crushed and mutilated beyond recognition. The girl had fallen down on the stone, and her father took her up in his arms and bore her away.

The youths who had taken the most pains to incite Leif to the perilous ascent now dared not lend a hand to pick him up; some were even unable to look at him. So the old people had to go forward. The eldest of them, as he took hold of the body, said: "It is very sad · but," he added, casting a look upward, "it is, after all, well that something hangs so high that it cannot be reached by every one."